REX TABBY
CAT DETECTIVE

POLICE

WHISKERVILLE
DETECTIVE

USA
1

DANIEL KIRK

ORCHARD BOOKS ★ NEW YORK
AN IMPRINT OF SCHOLASTIC INC.

LIBRARY OF CONGRESS CATALOGING-IN-PUBLICATION DATA

Kirk, Daniel. Rex Tabby / by Daniel Kirk.— 1st ed. p. cm.

Summary: Rex Tabby fights crime along with his partners, Simon Meeze and Frankie Fluff.

[1. Cats—Fiction. 2. Mystery and detective stories.] I. Title.

PZ7.K6339   Re 2004   [Fic]—dc22   2003018739

0-439-45286-4

10 9 8 7 6 5 4 3 2 1

04   05   06   07   08

Printed in the U.S.A.   23 · First edition, July 2004

The text was set in 15-pt. Perpetua

Book design by David Caplan

TO DON AND
CONNIE KIRK.
—D.K.

CHAPTER ONE
★ ★ ★
STOP IN THE NAME OF THE LAW!

Sit down, kids. I want you to listen, and listen good, 'cause I'm gonna tell you a story. It's a story about the battle between good and evil, between what's right and what's wrong, between the cats who wear a badge and the cats who break the law. It's a never-ending battle and it's going on right here and right now, on the streets of Whiskerville, U.S.A.

I'm Rex Tabby. Some have called me the greatest cat detective the world has ever known, and I'm about to tell you why. Meet Ma Manx and her kids, Rumpy and Stumpy. These furry felines are a family of catsters who let their appetite get the better of them. They're a gang of cats who went for a long walk — on the wrong side of the law.

It was four in the morning, a time when all good little kittens should be asleep. But the Manx kids weren't good, and they weren't tucked into their little beds, dreaming about butterflies and fuzzy balls of yarn. They were in the basement of the Fin-tastic Fish Company doing what they did best: stealing.

"Catch this, Ma!" laughed Rumpy and Stumpy as they lifted a big, wet tuna from the wooden crate and tossed it to their Ma.

"Keep them ocean delights coming!" shrieked Ma. She squeezed the fish into a huge blue suitcase with wheels. Ma always liked fast getaways.

"Make it snappy," Ma Manx screeched. "I'm not gonna stand here all night long!"

Ma's voice was like a pawful of nails dragged across a chalkboard. "Toss me a few more of that tasty tuna, and let's get out of here!"

Now, it just so happened that an alley cat called Hairball Harry had overheard the Manx gang bragging about the fish warehouse they were planning to rob that night. For the price of a can of sardines, Harry sold me the time and place.

The time? Four o'clock. The place? Right where we were, twitching our tails, waiting for the moment

when we could burst in and catch the Manx gang red-handed — or should I say, red-pawed, with a trunk full of stolen fish.

Simon Meeze was my partner and I called him Si, for short. Si and I and a street cop named Frankie Fluff were crouched behind the trash cans, waiting.

"Knock knock," whispered Frankie Fluff.

Frankie was as cute as a button, and you didn't want to mess with her. She may have been tough, but she loved knock-knock jokes. "Who's there?" I answered.

"Alex!" Frankie said.

"Alex who?"

"Alex 'plain it later!" Frankie giggled, covering her mouth with a rock-sized paw.

"You do that," I whispered, leaning down to the basement window.

"Hey, Rex," said Si, "that's the wrong window. Fin-tastic Fish Company is over here."

"Says who?" I asked.

"Simon says," said Si.

I crossed the alley and put my ear to the glass. "I knew it all along," I grumbled. "I was just testing you!"

Muffled laughter came from inside. Then one voice hit me. It was she — Ma Manx, the sneakiest and meanest cat of them all. "Let's go, kids!" Ma screeched, and slammed the suitcase shut.

I leaped up, rubbing my ear, and gave Frankie Fluff the signal.

Frankie hit the front door like a wall of bricks. She burst in, shouting, "Stop in the name of the law! This is the police! You are under arrest!"

But in the darkness Frankie stumbled, dropped her flashlight, and tumbled down a flight of stairs to the basement. How was I to know that these were the most rickety stairs the world has ever known? Si and I tumbled after Frankie and landed in a pile on the concrete floor.

"Run!" shouted Rumpy.

"Run!" shouted Stumpy. They tore past their mother as she groaned, dragging the trunk of stolen fish behind her. "You rotten cowards!" she howled. "Don't you dare leave me behind!"

Rumpy and Stumpy raced to the window and slipped out faster than Houdini from a pile of chains.

Frankie, Si, and I climbed to our feet. Rumpy and Stumpy may have escaped this time, but Ma Manx belonged to us. "Open the case, Ma," I ordered, "and Si, keep an eye on her. She's one tricky kitty!"

Ma popped open the lid, and a thousand eyes stared us right in the face — fish eyes, that is. Ma glared at us and let out an earsplitting howl that would have stopped an elephant in its tracks.

But as the greatest cat detective the world has ever known, I was prepared for the attack. "You're wasting your time, Ma," I shouted. "We're all wearing anti-shriek earplugs. Now, step away from the fish. You're going for a ride downtown!"

"Are ya gonna arrest me?" she hissed, and ripped my brand-new jacket with her sharp, painted claws.

I slapped on the cuffs. "You want to play, Ma? Now you're gonna have to pay!"

At the end of each chapter, I'll give you some questions, or a problem to solve. Simple? You bet. And this way you'll learn what it takes to become a real cat detective.

LESSON ONE

Check out the list below and pick out six things a cat detective uses to protect himself when he goes out to solve a crime.

watermelon

earplugs

houseplant

sunglasses

bowling ball

handkerchief

scratch-proof vest

skateboard

comic books

flea collar

rubber clown nose

billy club

squirt gun

rubber duckie

Now here are the answers I'm lookin' for. Let's see how you did!

EARPLUGS

You're going to want a pair of these if you ever run into a cat with a voice like Ma Manx. Even a tough guy like me needs to take care of those sensitive ears!

HANDKERCHIEF

Always keep a big one in your back pocket. You can dry off quickly and effectively if somebody splashes water on you. Cats really hate to get wet!

BILLY CLUB

Sometimes you get into a tussle with a sharp-toothed slimeball who won't come quietly, and you've got to be ready to play rough.

FLEA COLLAR

If you've ever been bitten by a flea, you'll know why you need one of these. You can't catch bad guys when you're busy scratchin' your armpit!

SCRATCH-PROOF VEST

When there's danger, you wear a scratch-proof vest. End of story. If you wanna come home to your family at the end of the night, you play it safe and wear the vest.

SQUIRT GUN

Did I say how much cats hate water? Just the threat of a good squirt will stop many a cat criminal in his evil tracks.

CHAPTER TWO
★ ★ ★
A BIG
FAT LIAR

We cuffed Ma Manx, threw her in the back of the police car, and drove her to the station house.

Now, when a criminal gets arrested and taken downtown, one of the first things we do is make them pose for a set of photographs we call "mug shots."

Ma Manx hissed and howled all the way to the camera. "I'm not ready," she cried. "Just let me go to the little girls' room to freshen up. Some lipstick and powder and I'll be lookin' good, baby!"

I figured that even the sneakiest mother cat the world has ever known deserved some privacy in the bathroom. But as the clock ticked, I wondered if I was right.

After twenty minutes I banged on the door and yelled, "Ma, you run out of toilet paper, or what?"

When I got no reply, I broke down the door and found her wedged into the window, half in and half out. "I was only tryin' to get a little fresh air," she screeched.

It took four strong police cats to pull her out again.

The captain came by to congratulate me and my boys on the arrest. "Tabby, you've done it again," he said.

"All in a day's work, Captain!" I answered.

"Too bad your day isn't over yet." The captain shook his head. "Two of Whiskerville's most dangerous criminals are still loose on the streets, and I don't want you to stop until the entire Manx gang is behind bars!"

"Just leave it to the greatest cat detective the world has ever known," I said. "Rex Tabby is on the case!"

It was time to get a fresh set of paw prints on Ma Manx. I took her by the arm and led her to the desk, then rolled her pudgy paw across the ink pad. "You broke my nail!" she hollered. "This is an outrage! You can't treat a lady this way! Call the doctor! Call the hospital! I feel faint! You're hurting me, STOP! STOP!"

"Knock knock," Frankie Fluff said to Ma.

"Who's there?" she answered.

"Moose," he said.

"Moose who?"

Frankie leaned in close and answered, "Moose you be so annoying?"

"I want my lawyer," Ma said.

"Your lawyer is afraid of you," I answered. "In fact, every lawyer in Whiskerville is afraid of you. Now, why don't you just cut to the chase and tell us where your kittens are hiding. We're going to nail the three of you for that robbery."

"Robbery?" Ma Manx cried. "That was no robbery. We was just lookin' at the fish! I brought my darlings on a little field trip, on account of Rumpy and Stumpy learning about fish in school. Is it a crime for a mother to try to help her children get a good education?"

My whiskers twitched. Somehow, I had the feeling that Ma Manx might not be telling the truth. Could she have been the greatest liar the world has ever known? I decided to call her bluff.

"Listen, Ma," I said, "you're talkin' to Rex Tabby, and nobody makes a fool out of me. Make it easy on yourself and confess!"

"Rumpy and Stumpy are good kids," Ma said, and smiled. "They never hurt nobody, or did nothin' wrong."

I pulled out a file on the Manx gang that was nearly as thick as a phone book. Inside was a wanted poster of Rumpy and Stumpy, and I held it up for Ma to see. "Tell me where your little angels are hiding!" I shouted. "Let me round 'em up before the mess they're in gets any deeper."

"My angels!" Ma cried. "They look so adorable, I could just eat 'em right up!"

Ma lunged forward, snatched the poster out of my paw with her sharp yellow teeth, and swallowed the pictures in one gulp. "Answering all them questions worked up my appetite!" she purred.

Ma was tough; tougher than a frozen fish stick. If I couldn't get her to talk, nobody could! "Ma," I said, shaking my head, "we've got a jail cell downstairs that's just your size. I'm sure some time behind bars will help you remember where Rumpy and Stumpy are hiding."

"I'm sure of one thing," Ma shrieked as my team dragged her off to her cell. "You're going to be very sorry you ever messed with Ma Manx!"

Ma was right. I was already sorry.

I never cared much for games, but if Rumpy and Stumpy were going to play hide-and-seek, I was going to play along. And I was going to win.

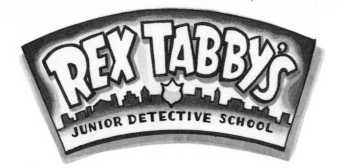

Ma Manx is a big fat liar. But sometimes it's hard to know for sure if somebody's telling you the truth, or dealing you a pack of lies.

Answer these statements true or false, and see if you've got what it takes to be a real, live lie detector.

LESSON TWO
TRUE OR FALSE

1. A liar always looks into your eyes when telling a lie.
2. A liar often crosses his arms or legs when telling a lie.
3. A liar often talks very slowly.

ANSWERS

1. **False.** Most often, liars will look *anywhere* but in your eyes. They're afraid you will know they are lying!

2. **True.** Some liars just can't sit still. They're afraid you know they are lying, and they want to get away.

3. **False.** Liars usually talk faster than normal, hoping you won't notice they have lied!

CHAPTER THREE
★ ★ ★
ON THE RUN

Ma Manx may have been safely behind bars, but her kittens, Rumpy and Stumpy, were on the run. Where could they be? How could we find them?

"Say, I've got an idea," said my partner, Simon, getting up from his desk. "Let's pretend that we're Rumpy and Stumpy, and maybe that will help us figure out what they'll do next!"

"Rex Tabby, the greatest detective the world has ever known, does not pretend to be a bad guy, Si!"

"I think we should give it a try," said Si.

"Says who?" said I.

"Simon says," said Si.

"Oh, all right," I grumbled, "when you put it that way. If I were a small fry, where would I go, and why? I'd turn myself in to the police. I'd crawl on my hands and knees to the judge and beg for mercy."

"They're just kids," said Si. "Kids go to the playground. The candy shop."

"The candy shop!" I exclaimed. "Yummy! Bring the patrol car around and we'll take a ride!"

At Silky Sam's Sweets I bagged a jumbo box of Minnow Mints, the greatest candy the world has ever known. Si scored a sack of Trout Tarts, but Rumpy and Stumpy were nowhere in sight. Strike one for the good guys.

Next stop, Puss' n' Boots Memorial Playground, City Park. I pulled Rumpy and Stumpy's wanted poster from my jacket pocket as Detective Meeze and I crossed the grass. "Hey, kids!" I called to a group of youngsters climbing on a cat-apult. "Have any of you kittens ever laid eyes on these two troublemakers?"

"Wow!" the kittens cried. "Cool! A wanted poster! Can we get pictures like that of us?"

"You'd better hope not," said Si.

"Now, look carefully. Do these two ever come around here?"

"They look like a couple of stinkers," one kitten cried.

"I haven't seen faces like that since Halloween!"

"Hey, what about our reward?" another kitten asked.

"Reward? What reward?" I said.

"Our reward for cooperating with the police! Our reward! Our reward!" They all began jumping up and down like kangaroos on a mattress.

"Does anybody here like Trout Tarts?" asked Si. "Or Minnow Mints?"

"Minnow Mints! Minnow Mints!" they squealed together.

Si glanced at me, and I shrugged my shoulders. "Come on, Rex," my partner begged.

"Oh, all right," I grumbled. "Here, just take the whole bag!" I stalked back to the patrol car angry, hungry, and exhausted. "Strike two for the good guys," I said.

"Rounding up the rest of the Manx gang may be harder than we thought," sighed Si.

"Those kids are criminal masterminds," I grumbled. "They could be the cleverest kittens the world has ever known! I'll bet they're putting their tricky little heads together right now, plotting their next move!"

Meanwhile, Rumpy and Stumpy were keeping busy. "Should we watch some more cartoons?" Stumpy asked his sister. "Or should we jump on the bed some more?"

"Let's do both!" shouted Rumpy, and they jumped until the springs shot out of their mattress like daffodils in the month of May.

"I don't feel good," said Rumpy.

"I don't feel good, either," said Stumpy.

"But I feel worse than you do," said Rumpy.

"No, you don't!" said Stumpy.

"Yes, I do!" shouted Rumpy.

"No, you don't!" hollered Stumpy.

And the kittens toppled to the floor, scratching and wrestling until they were nearly too tired to move.

"I miss Ma," said Rumpy.

"I miss her, too," said Stumpy. "I miss her more than you do."

"No, you don't. I miss her more than you!" shouted Rumpy, and the kittens rolled on the floor, knocking over their TV, a pair of lamps, and a framed picture of Ma Manx, scratching and biting and wrestling until they fell asleep.

It was getting late, but Detective Meeze and I went to the docks to meet Hairball Harry. Perhaps he had the information we were looking for.

"Let's not beat around the bush, Hairball," I said. "We're lookin' for Rumpy and Stumpy Manx, and we hear you can tell us where they are."

"Oh, yeah?" said Hairball. "Says who?"

"Simon says," said Si.

Si always seemed to know just what to say.

"Well, in that case," Hairball whispered, "maybe I know a cat who knows a cat who knows something."

Hairball sent us to see a cat named Dirtball Dave, who sent us to see a cat named Screwball Sue, who sent us to a cat named Slimeball Sam.

"I know I've seen 'em around somewhere," he said, "but my memory is a little foggy on the fine points."

As the greatest cat detective the world has ever known, I knew just what Slimeball needed to jog his memory. I grabbed his tail and gave a little squeeze.

Slimeball was a good boy. He told us about a cave behind the bowling alley on the outskirts of town, a place he said the Manx gang called home.

Si and I jumped into the patrol car, and with our siren screaming we headed south on Shark Street. I could feel it in my whiskers. We were on the right track, and the trail was still warm from the hot little feet of Rumpy and Stumpy Manx.

We detectives use a lot of words that are special to our line of work. "Cop slang" is what we call it, and hidden in the list of words below are ten cop slang terms for "jail." See if you can pick 'em out!

LESSON THREE

Find ten words below that mean the same thing as "jail."

sandbox	stir	g-joint
dirty diaper	teepee	big house
cootie catch	slammer	walls
jitterbox	steel trap	keep
bootlick	cage	can
stinky sock	drum	closet
hoosegow	igloo	

Here's Rex Tabby's list of some of the colorful terms that cops and robbers use for the word "jail."

g-joint	hoosegow	slammer
can	stir	keep
drum	big house	cage

There may be a lot of different ways to say "jail," but there's only one thing you need to know about jail: Stay out of it!

CHAPTER FOUR
★ ★ ★
A BIRD
IN THE HAND

Lying on a bed of old newspapers and Kitty Litter, the twins woke up with their stomachs growling like a pair of angry pumas. "Ma?" called Stumpy. "I'm hungry!"

"Ma's in jail, DUH!" spat Rumpy as she crawled to the cupboard to look for some breakfast. "There's no food in the house!" she cried, brushing away a stuffed mouse and an empty box of Liver Lumps. "Stumpy, we're going to starve! Unless . . ."

"Listen," Rumpy said, "I've got a brilliant idea. Just 'cause Ma's in jail doesn't mean she can't feed us breakfast. There must be lots of food in jail. Let's go there and get Ma to hand some chow over to us!"

"Are you nuts?" Stumpy cried. "If we show up at the jailhouse, they'll arrest us for sure!"

"No, really!" his sister answered. "We'll take off our disguises, and nobody will know who we are! Without these dumb burglar masks, everybody will think we're just a cute pair of kittens. Besides, the jail cells have their windows in the back. If we're careful, the coppers won't even see us."

The sun came up over the quiet streets of Whiskerville as Rumpy and Stumpy made their way across town. Soon they came to the rear entrance of the jail. There they stood in the grass, mewing pitifully, until a familiar face popped up from behind barred windows.

Ma Manx rubbed her eyes. "Is that my babies, without their disguises on? Come to rescue their mama? Listen, Manx children always wear a mask! But I'll forgive you, this one time. Now, did you bring a nice sharp file? Or a saw? Get movin', kittens. Mama's itchin' for her freedom!"

"Ma," said Rumpy, "It's 6:30 A.M. and we don't have anything to eat! We were hoping you'd get us some breakfast and pass it out to us through the bars."

"You think I have a KITCHEN in here?" Ma Manx shrieked. "If you're so hungry, go out and catch yourselves something to eat. And when your bellies are nice and full, get back here and SAVE ME!"

"I never caught my own food before," cried Stumpy as they stomped down the street. "Ma always took good care of us!"

"Hey!" whispered Rumpy. "Look up in the tree, in that branch over the apartment building, and tell me what you see!"

"Duh, it's a bird!" said Stumpy.

"That's no ordinary bird," hissed Rumpy. "That's breakfast, wearing a beak! Climb up there and catch him!"

"YOU climb up there and catch him," said Stumpy. "I'm afraid of heights!"

"Scaredy-cat!" his sister growled. "We'll both go up the tree. You know what they say. 'The early cat catches the bird'!"

"I want the wings," Stumpy whispered, licking his lips. "They taste best."

"SSSSSSHHHH!" answered Rumpy. "Keep quiet, or you'll be lucky if you get a mouthful of feathers. Now, climb out there and grab him!"

The twins slowly inched their way along the branch. Then, with a cry, Stumpy lost his grip, and a claw slipped on the bark. "HELP!" he hollered.

The sparrow gave a little tweet and flapped into the air. "I've got him!" screamed Stumpy, and she leaped over her brother to catch the bird.

CRRRRAAAACK! went the branch.

Rumpy and Stumpy clawed at the air, tumbling down and down. A flock of birds watched from the branches of the tree as the kittens fell, and they clapped their little wings and laughed.

With a loud CRASH, Rumpy and Stumpy burst through the glass panes of a rooftop skylight. They tumbled to the carpet of the apartment below, and scrambled to their feet. "Who's in there?" yelled a tired voice from the bedroom.

"Uh," said Rumpy, thinking fast, "it's just Santa Claws, coming down your chimney with a sack full of presents, so stay where you are!"

"But it's summertime!" answered the old cat. "Santa Claws doesn't come until winter!"

"Let's get out of here," whispered Stumpy, knocking over a chair and heading for the door.

"Let's get out of here," whispered Rumpy, grabbing Stumpy's paw, knocking over a table, and heading for the kitchen.

When the old cat in the striped pajamas finally peered around the corner, armed with a broom and ready to strike, he found the back door of his apartment flung open.

The robbers were gone, but cans of sardines were strewn on the counter and a box of chow was spilled across the floor.

With trembling paws, he picked up the phone and dialed 911.

Minutes later, help arrived with a badge, a note-book, and a bad joke. "Knock knock," said Frankie Fluff, smiling as she stood in the doorway.

"Who's there?" answered the confused old cat.

"Oliver," giggled Frankie, covering her mouth with a paw.

"Oliver? But I called the police!" cried the victim.

"No, no, it's a joke!" said Frankie. "You're supposed to ask, 'Oliver who?'"

"Oliver who?" asked the old cat.

"Oliver town there are bad guys who are up to no good, but don't worry, because the Whiskerville Police are on the job!"

"Knock knock?" said the old cat, shaking his head. "Say, are you going to ask me what the robbers looked like?"

"Oh, goodie." Frankie grinned. "Is this a joke?"

"This is not a joke," shouted the cat. "It was 7:00 A.M. I remember hearing the church bells, and then I heard a loud crash. They destroyed all my prized possessions."

Frankie apologized. Then she wrote the old cat's story down in her notebook. Then she apologized again, and made a list of all the things the victim claimed the robbers stole or broke. It was a long list. Then Frankie tipped her hat, apologized one final time, and left for the station house. "Sheesh," she muttered to herself, "some cats just have no sense of humor!"

Believe it or not, some cats don't tell the whole truth to the police, even when they are looking for our help. Take that cat in striped pajamas, for example. Some of the things he claimed were broken by Rumpy and Stumpy were already damaged before the Manx kittens ever crossed his path.

LESSON FOUR

Look at the pictures below and see if you can prove which one of the objects the cat lied about.

If you guessed the clock, go ahead and step to the head of the class!

There are no clues to help us with the other objects, but take a look at the face of the clock. The hands stopped turning when the clock was broken at 2:05. Rumpy and Stumpy didn't enter the old cat's apartment until 7 A.M. So they couldn't have broken the clock!

CHAPTER FIVE
★★★
HOT ON
THE TRAIL

Behind the bowling alley, Si and I met a cat named Gutterball Gus. When I greased his palm with a fresh dollar bill, Gus told us about the tree house at the far end of the swamp, where the Manx family had their hideout.

We rolled up the legs of our trousers. Then we grit our teeth, and waded into a world of trouble.

"Keep your eyes open for a path of dry land through this swamp," said Si.

"I'll give it a try," I answered. "I hate getting wet. I'd rather be dry. Out here you can drown in the wink of an eye."

"Rex, look out for that snake!" Si let out a cry.

I jumped like there were springs attached to my feet, and with a huge *SPLASH* I disappeared beneath a thick layer of pond scum. When I sputtered to the surface, frogs plopped from my shoulders, and mosquitoes buzzed around my ears, but there was no snake in sight.

"Sorry, Rex," Si laughed weakly, "There wasn't a snake after all — it was just a branch sticking out of some mud over here. Better safe than sorry, don't you think?"

Si grabbed the stick and pulled hard. When it was

loose, he offered me the muddy end, and I took hold

and paddled over to drier land.

Suddenly a lump of fur shot from the hole in the mound of dirt where the stick had been. "MEE-OWCH!" Si hollered as one critter after another scurried out of the opening.

"Let's get out of here!" I shouted, and we bolted through the muck and slime. A whole family of angry beavers tore after us, hot and bothered that Si had pulled a big stick from the base of their dam.

Si and I scrambled onto a patch of dry land and picked up speed. Then we raced through the woods

until we'd left the beavers far behind. "Rex," my partner huffed and puffed, "I think we lost 'em. But I think we're lost, too!"

"Rex Tabby, the greatest cat detective the world has ever known," I gasped for breath, "usually doesn't get lost!"

I was wet from head to paws. "That was a close call!" I exclaimed. "Did you get a look at those beaver teeth?"

"Yeah!" said Si. "And their tails were flapping mad."

Just then we came to a tree house with a big sign that read WARNING! KEEP AWAY! Could this be the secret hideout of the Manx gang?

"HEY, YOU IN THERE, COME OUT WITH YOUR PAWS IN THE AIR!" I shouted. "IT'S THE WHISKERVILLE POLICE!"

Well, it could have been the Manx hideout, but it wasn't. A little old hermit cat crawled down the ladder. "Say, old-timer," I asked him, "is this your tree house?"

"Free mouse?" he cried. "There's no free mouse in these woods. You'll have to catch your own mice around here!"

Si gave it a try. "Listen, sir, could you help us? We're trying to locate the home of Ma Manx and her kittens, RUMPY AND STUMPY!"

"Grumpy and Lumpy?" the cat answered. "You may be a police cat, but watch who you're callin' names!"

"Ahhh, it's useless." I tried one more time. "WE ARE LOOKING FOR THE MANX KITTENS!" I shouted. "MANX!"

"Manx?" he answered. "Are you looking for the Manx family? They live in the tree house just up the road. You can't miss it!"

We dashed along the road until we spied a roof peeking up from behind black and drooping pines. Then we tiptoed toward the tree house, ready for a showdown.

Suddenly a pair of dark and slippery shapes shimmied down the ladder at the back of the tree house. "Stop in the name of the law!" I shouted. "You're under arrest!"

"We haven't done anything wrong!" cried our captives, slinking forward with their paws in the air.

"Rumpy and Stumpy Manx, your days of crime are over," I said, getting out my handcuffs.

"But we're not the Manx family," one of them protested. "We're the Mink family — Jumpy and Thumpy Mink!"

"Yeah, well, I'm Rex Tabby, the greatest cat detective the world has ever known, and you can't fool me."

"But Rex," said Si, pulling at my coattails, "these characters don't look anything like Rumpy and Stumpy. I think we've got the wrong guys!"

"You've got to remember that these criminals are experts at the art of disguise," I grumbled. "They know how to make themselves look like anything — that's why they are so hard to catch!"

I nudged our captives along the dirt trail. "Now, don't make any trouble. When we get to our car at the other end of the swamp," I sighed, "we're all gonna take a nice ride downtown."

I'll be ready to join you as soon as I get some of this mud off my shoe. The swamp, as you have seen, is a gross, stinking, horrible place. It's home to dozens of critters you don't want to meet, and cats who ought to know better than to live there.

LESSON FIVE

Get out your pencils (unless this is a library book you're holding in your sticky little paws, in which case I want you to use your finger!) and see if you can travel the maze from the bowling alley to the Mink brothers' tree house at the other end. Don't forget to wear your boots!

Congratulations, kids, you made it. Now let me rub some medicine on those mosquito bites. If the itching isn't driving you crazy, I'll be waiting for you in Chapter Six!

CHAPTER SIX
★ ★ ★
MASTERS OF DISGUISE

Behind a row of trash cans in an alley as dirty as an earthworm's underwear, Stumpy sat frowning at his sister. "If you were going to steal cans of cat food, Rumpy, why didn't you steal a can opener, too?"

"I can't think of everything," she muttered. "I'm so hungry, my brain is all fuzzy. Besides, you've got brains of your own, haven't you? You didn't steal anything!"

"I know," said Stumpy sadly. "Maybe I'm just not cut out for a life of crime."

"Don't be silly," Rumpy answered. "Ma always said we were born to be bad. You just need a little more practice, that's all! Now, be a bad boy and try to open up one of those cans with your teeth. Yours are much sharper than mine!"

"OW!" Stumpy cried, chomping down on the edge of the metal can.

"Bite harder!" ordered Rumpy. "And don't make so much noise. I think I hear something!"

Along the wall, a fat black rat scampered over a pile of garbage. He took one look at the Manx kittens, let out a terrified squeak, and dashed for cover.

"Let's get him!" shouted Rumpy, and the Manx twins leaped to their feet and crashed through the alley in hot pursuit.

"There he goes!" Rumpy hollered as the rat rounded a corner and slipped through a hole near a door marked WHISKERVILLE COSTUME SHOP.

"Don't let him get away!" Rumpy cried, and Stumpy flung open the door of the shop and raced inside.

"Hey, what do you kids think you're doing?" shouted the cat behind the counter.

The kittens tore down the aisle. "Mister, there's a rat in your store!" Rumpy answered. "And we're going to catch him!"

"A RAT?!" screamed the clerk. "A rat doesn't belong in my store — it belongs on my dinner plate!"

The rat made a sharp turn and fled down the basement steps. As the kittens were about to follow, the big cat leaped in front of them and dove down the stairs. "Darn," sighed Stumpy. "There goes our breakfast!"

"Don't be so sure about that." Rumpy smiled, shutting the basement door and carefully turning the lock. "While the cat's away, the kittens will play!"

"I don't want to play," moaned Stumpy. "I want to eat!"

"Let's see if there's any food in this joint," said his sister, quickly looking around. "What's this? Right here on the shelf — candy!"

Stumpy ripped off the wrapper and shoved the hard, pink lump into his mouth. "Ugh, this tastes terrible," he groaned, slobber running down his chin.

"Well, look here on the label, you oaf," said Rumpy. "This is trick candy, and it's made out of rubber. Here, try some of this gum instead!"

Stumpy tore open the package. "AAAAH!" he cried as he began to chew. "My mouth is burning! This is hot pepper gum! Rumpy, you tricked me!"

Rumpy clipped a plastic flower onto her blouse. "It's just a joke," she said. "Why don't you sniff this pretty flower I found?"

"I don't want to smell your stupid flower. I need water!" Stumpy cried, racing around in circles.

"I told you to take a sniff," Rumpy said, forcing the daisy into her brother's face. She squeezed a little rubber ball at the end of a cord that led to the daisy, and a spray of water shot out of the flower and into her brother's teary eyes.

"HA-HA-HA!" she laughed, and Stumpy coughed with relief as Bumpy squirted water into his open mouth.

"That's pretty funny," she said. "I think I'll take this trick home with me, along with a jar or two of itching powder, and this gum that turns your tongue blue!"

In the basement, there was more banging and crashing than a fireworks display on the Fourth of July. "He isn't much of a rat-catcher, is he?" smirked Rumpy. "Let's see if there's any real food to eat around here."

"Jackpot!" cried Stumpy as he peered at a shelf below the cash register. "I found a sack of Flounder Flakes. Do you think that cat would mind if we ate some?"

"Those flakes belong to us now," answered Rumpy, snatching the sack from her brother's claws. "Don't forget, that rat was as good as ours, until the cat in the basement stole him from us.

"Besides, we're supposed to be bad. If you're given the choice between right and wrong, choose wrong every time. It's the right thing to do!"

When Rumpy's and Stumpy's bellies were stuffed with Flounder Flakes, they sat and listened to the racket coming from the basement. "I'll put my money on the rat to win this contest," Stumpy burped.

"You don't have any money," said Rumpy. "But while the battle is still raging, we should find out if there's anything else here to steal."

"Look at this!" Stumpy laughed, pulling a rubber clown mask over his face. "With this mask on, I could fool other cats into thinking I was nice. Then, once they trust me, you could rob them!"

"Nobody trusts a clown," said Rumpy as she put on a black eye patch and waved a plastic cutlass. "Ahoy, matey," she cried, "tell me where you've buried the treasure, or I'll make you walk the plank!"

Stumpy climbed into a suit that had KNIGHT IN ARMOR printed on the package. "Don't worry, fair damsel," he said, peering through the helmet, "for I will save you from the horrible dragon!"

"Shut up," Rumpy said, looking out from the eyes of a green rubber head. "I am the dragon!"

"Check this out!" laughed Stumpy, pulling on a big overcoat and a heavy mask. "It's a detective disguise. Now I look just like that horrible ugly cat who arrested our Ma!"

"I like the handcuffs that come with that costume!" purred Rumpy.

Suddenly the rattling and banging in the basement stopped. "Gotcha!" came a voice from below.

"Uh-oh," cried Stumpy, "it's time for us to leave. When that cat comes up the stairs and finds out we locked him in, he isn't going to be very happy!"

"What's going on? HELP! Somebody, let me OUT of here!" the cat hollered from behind the basement door, but there was no one upstairs to hear his cries. Rumpy and Stumpy were racing down the street, with bags of tricks and disguises tucked under their arms.

"Stumpy," whispered Rumpy. "I've got a great idea. Wait 'til you hear what we're gonna do with these costumes."

You might say there was a lot to look at in the Whiskerville Costume Shop. In fact, you might say that the place was packed to the rafters with junk! It would be hard to know if a few things turned up missing. Hard, yes — but not impossible. Let's test your powers of observation.

LESSON SIX

Look carefully at the details in this picture. Come on, now —
you can look harder than that! When you're done, turn the page.

Here's a list of objects you might find in a really cool costume shop. Without looking back at the picture, try to remember which of these items were NOT in the scene that you studied.

princess dress	magic book	rubber sandwich
gorilla mask	rubber rat	black soap
giant glasses	moose head	itching powder
vampire fangs	skeleton	pirate flag
top hat	shoes with toes	
burglar mask	giant bugs	

ANSWERS:
GIANT GLASSES
VAMPIRE FANGS

CHAPTER SEVEN
★ ★ ★
PULLING
THE PLUG

Back at Police Headquarters, it was time for a lineup. Six characters stood in a row beneath the glare of a spotlight. Two of them were the punks who called themselves Jumpy and Thumpy Mink, and the other four were guys from the station house who got paid

to stand in line and look tough. On the wall facing our lineup was a big picture window. Instead of glass, the window held a two-way mirror.

On the other side of the mirror were Officer Frankie Fluff, Si Meeze, and yours truly, Detective Rex Tabby. Joining us for the occasion were the cat in striped pajamas from the apartment building, and the clerk from the costume shop, who had broken down the basement door and called the police. Now the two crime victims were here to try to identify the cats who had robbed them.

"Knock knock," said Frankie Fluff.

"Oh, no, here we go again," moaned the cat in striped pajamas.

"Who's there?" asked the store clerk.

"Juicy," giggled Frankie.

"Juicy who?" asked the clerk.

"Juicy the guys who robbed you?" Frankie grinned, pointing at the characters on the other side of the glass window.

"You can see them, but they can't see you," I said. "Look carefully and tell us if the criminals who hurt you are standing in the lineup."

"Uh, wait a minute," said Frankie. "According to

my report, the characters we're looking for are Manx kittens, and they don't have tails. All of the cats in this lineup have tails, so they can't be Rumpy and Stumpy!"

"Don't be so sure about that," I explained. "The Manx kittens are experts at the art of disguise. Those might be fake tails you're looking at. Here, I'll show you!"

With that, I flung open the door, walked into the other room, and began pulling the tails of the suspects in the lineup. "If these tails aren't real, I guarantee that two of them are going to come off in my paw!"

Well, you've never heard such howling and yowling in your whole life. Lucky for me, I was still wearing my anti-shriek earplugs, and the racket didn't bother me at all. But not a single tail came off the backsides of the suspects we had in our lineup.

With no evidence to hold them, we had to let Thumpy and Jumpy Mink go. "Stay out of trouble," I warned them. "We'll be watching you!"

It looked like Rumpy and Stumpy Manx were still on the loose. "Si," I said to my partner, "this case is going nowhere. Bring the car around. Let's head back to the candy store and see if Rumpy and Stumpy have been there since our last visit."

A bag of Minnow Mints and a sack of Trout Tarts later, my partner and I stood chewing happily outside Silky Sam's Sweets. We'd learned nothing about Rumpy and Stumpy's whereabouts, but at least we had lots of candy to make us feel better. "Where to next?" asked Si, his mouth stuffed with treats.

"We haven't been to the video arcade lately," I said. "Let's swing by there and see if anybody's laid eyes on the Manx kittens."

At the arcade, kids stood hunched and hypnotized before the flashing lights of their favorite games. "Ah," I sighed, "the place hasn't changed much from when I was the Whiskerville Space Cats champion!"

"LISTEN UP, EVERYBODY," my partner hollered, holding up the old photographs of Rumpy and Stumpy. "WE'RE FROM THE WHISKERVILLE POLICE! HAVE ANY OF YOU SEEN THESE TWO KITTENS?"

But nobody was in the mood to pay much attention to anything that didn't have flashing lights or electronic noise blasting out of its speakers.

"Check out the other side of the room, Si!" I shouted. "When this punk here is done playing Space Cats, I'll ask him some questions."

I stood over the kitten's shoulder and watched him play. "Not bad, kid, not bad," I said. "Of course, I used to be pretty good at this game. I once shot all five thousand asteroids out of their orbits in under ten seconds with nothing but a level-one Kitty-Litter laser cannon."

"That's impossible." The kid looked up. "Nobody can do that."

"Step aside, lad." I smiled. "And watch a master at his art."

I took off my jacket and draped it over a chair. Then I rolled up my sleeves, nudged the kid out of my way, and dropped a quarter into the slot.

Across the room, Si went from game to game, trying to snag somebody's attention long enough to show them the pictures. "Leave us alone, mister," the players complained. "Can't you see we're busy?"

Meanwhile, I was on top of the world. I was a Master of the Universe. I was blasting alien dog ships out of the sky, and the numbers on the scoreboard were spinning faster than a hamster in a plastic wheel.

Soon, every cat in the joint was crowded around and staring over my shoulder as I entered level ten. I locked in my laser beam on the evil Sir Loin and his dripping doodie-dogs of Andromeda.

I was heading fast for a world record — when suddenly my cat blaster wilted on the screen like a melted crayon, and my game blacked out like the inside of an anthill during a solar eclipse.

I spun around. There was my partner, Si Meeze, standing by the empty wall socket with the plug to the Space Cats game dangling from his paw.

"All right," hollered Si. "Now that I have your attention, I am going to show you a picture of two very dangerous criminals known as Rumpy and Stumpy Manx. If any one of you has seen these kittens or knows where they might be, I expect you to cooperate and tell us what you know."

"What's that guy talking about?" a voice rose from the crowd.

"I don't know," said another, "but I'm going home."

"Yeah, me, too," complained a third, and all the cats began shuffling out the door.

"Si," I said to my partner, "before you ruined my game, I was this close to frying the evil Sir Loin."

"Well done," said Si. "But don't forget what we're here for!"

I grit my teeth. "Yeah, yeah, Rumpy and Stumpy, Stumpy and Rumpy. Those two are really beginning to get on my nerves!"

A voice crackled over the police radio. "Calling Detectives Tabby and Meeze, we have received a phone call from someone who wants to reveal the whereabouts of Rumpy and Stumpy Manx. Report to Police Headquarters immediately. Over!"

It began to look as if this case was nearly over and suddenly I was feeling pretty happy. As happy as a pig in mud. As happy as Dracula at the blood bank. As happy as . . . well, I should have saved a little happiness for later. Because, as they say in Whiskerville, it ain't over 'til it's over.

Every kid in Rex Tabby's Junior Detective School has to learn how to operate a real police lineup. And each and every one of you needs to be able to spot a bad guy and remember what he looks like, in case you see him again.

LESSON SEVEN

Take a close look at the troublemaker you see in this picture.
Note everything you can about his face and his outfit, before
he runs away with your brand-new sneakers or watch. OOPS!
Too late. Somebody stop that crook!

Whew! Thanks to some fancy police work, we caught the thief and brought him down to headquarters.

Here he is now, in a lineup with five other guys that look a lot like him. Can you spot the real villain?

Number Four is the bad guy we were looking for. Let's put that creep behind bars, and move ahead to Chapter Eight!

THE MEETING PLACE

The captain's eyes were as big as saucers of milk as Detective Meeze and I strode into the station.

"REX!" he cried. "While you were gone, somebody called and said he had information about Rumpy and Stumpy Manx — but he wants to talk only to you! He said he's gonna call back in thirty minutes, and it's — "

BRRRRRINNNNNNG! The phone on my desk rang as loudly as an alarm clock on the first day of school. I jumped like I'd sat on a tack, and grabbed the receiver. "Detective Tabby speaking," I said.

"Now, listen, Tabby, and listen good," the voice on the other end of the line snarled. "We know — that is, I know — where the Manx kittens are hiding, but this information is expensive. . . . You're going to have to come up with a big reward!"

"Keep talking," I said, my teeth clenched like a vise.

"Meet me at the end of the pier behind the Whiskerville Amusement Park, just before closing time," the voice said, "and I'll tell you what you want to know. Bring along a big sack of chocolate-covered Minnow Mints, and come alone. If there's any sign of another cop with you, we'll disappear and you'll never find us — I mean, you'll never find the Manx kittens again — 'cause when they hide, they hide good!"

I hung up the phone, never suspecting the truth.

Not even I, Rex Tabby, the greatest cat detective of them all, could ever have guessed that Rumpy Manx was the mysterious cat on the other end of the line! She and her brother, Stumpy, were setting a trap . . . and we were about to take the bait.

Another day of fun was winding down at the Whiskerville Amusement Park. It was a shabby place thrown together from rusted metal and half-rotten wood, smelling of damp Kitty Litter and stale cotton candy. The park sprawled across a dirty strip of blacktop down by the docks.

Two shadowy figures snuck through a hole in the chain-link fence that surrounded the park. They dragged a sack of clothing behind an empty storage shed, and set to work.

"I don't see why I couldn't be the one on top," Stumpy Manx complained to his sister as she climbed onto his shoulders. Rumpy struggled to keep her balance and pull the heavy detective's trench coat around the two of them.

"You're the boy," she snapped at him. "You're bigger than me, and stronger. You should be flattered that I am letting you have such an important job."

"I'm not much bigger," whined Stumpy, "and if I were on top, then I could do the talking, and my voice is much deeper and scarier than yours."

Rumpy pulled the ugly rubber mask down over her face, popped the hat on her head, and pulled the brim low. "With Ma gone," she growled, "I'm the brains of this outfit, see? Just walk the way I tell you to, and before you know it, our bellies will be full of candy and the keys to the police station will be safe in our pocket."

"Let me get this straight," Stumpy's muffled voice said from inside the coat. "We're going to overpower Detective Tabby, grab the candy and his keys, then race back to the police station and sneak in?"

"You've been paying attention," Rumpy replied. "I'm proud of you! In this disguise we stole from the costume shop, we look just like a real detective. Once we're inside the police station, the other cats will never suspect a thing."

"They'll probably think we're Rex Tabby!" Stumpy shook with laughter.

"We're not that ugly," Rumpy replied. "And hold still, fish-face, or I'll fall off your shoulders. Once we get the keys, all we have to do is sneak down into the jail. Then we open up the lock to Ma's cell and lead her right out the front door! If anybody says anything, we'll just explain that Ma's been transferred to the State Prison in Purrtown. It'll be a piece of cake."

"Don't mention cake," Stumpy groaned. "I'm so hungry, I can't see straight!"

"You can't see because you're inside the coat!" his sister cried. "Just do what you're told, and everything will be fine."

"Just do what you're told, and everything will be fine," I said to my partner, Si Meeze, and Officer Frankie Fluff as we sped down the freeway. "I've got this meeting all figured out."

"I don't mean to pry," said Si, "but didn't that cat on the phone say that he didn't want you to bring anyone along with you?"

"That I won't deny," said I. "But I'm not the kind of guy who'd put his life in danger without having some help nearby."

"I guess I'm not the only sly one," said Si.

I gave no reply as I steered the car into the nearly empty parking lot outside the Whiskerville Amusement Park. "There was something about that cat on the phone that I just didn't like," I said. "When we get to the pier, I want the two of you to hide just out of sight, and make sure there's nothing fishy going on. Once I get the information about Rumpy and Stumpy, I'll say the word 'tuna.' That will be your signal to rush in, and then we'll arrest him."

"Arrest him for what?" asked Frankie Fluff, who was polishing off a box of anchovy doughnuts as she climbed out of the backseat.

"Give me a minute and I'll think of something," I said.

I was just pushing my way through the turnstile when the cat in the ticket booth stopped me. "Uh uh uh," he sneered, "where do you think you're going? That'll be sixty tickets for the three of you, buster."

I flashed my badge. "We're Whiskerville Detectives, here on police business," I said.

"HA!" The cat laughed bitterly. "I've heard that one before. You cops just like to ride the roller coaster. That'll cost you sixty tickets. If you want to play, then you've got to pay!"

"Yeah," I said, forking over the dough for the tickets, "I've heard that one before, too."

It was nearly closing time. "Try your luck, friends! Three balls for a buck," a cat called out from one of the game tents. "Win a stuffed tiger for your sweetie!"

"Which way to the pier, Rex?" Si asked me as we walked across the trash-strewn lot.

"Straight ahead," I whispered. "Now, stay out of sight — there's somebody out there. Time for Rex Tabby to go to work!"

Rumpy and Stumpy Manx may not be very big, but they are big liars — just like their Ma. Here's Part Two of our test on how to tell if somebody is telling you a big fat lie!

LESSON EIGHT
TRUE OR FALSE

1. A liar sometimes covers his or her mouth with a paw when telling a lie.

2. A liar will appear very serious and will never laugh or smile while lying.

3. A liar will sometimes shake his head NO when answering YES to a question, and shake his head YES when answering NO to a question.

ANSWERS

1. **True.** Covering up your mouth is a pretty good way to hide the truth, even if the words you speak are an obvious lie.

2. **False.** Liars often laugh or smile when they lie, to fool you into thinking they are your friends.

3. **True.** The shake of the head will often reveal the truth, even when the words coming from the mouth are false.

CHAPTER NINE
★ ★ ★
SHOWDOWN

The amusement park was nearly deserted. One lone figure stood in the lamplight at the end of the pier.

"Get down!" I grabbed Detective Meeze and Officer Fluff and pushed them into the shadows. As luck would have it, we were standing next to a row of cars on a track outside the entrance of a ride called The Howl of Horror.

"Hide in one of these cars," I whispered, "and don't come out until I say the secret word!"

Slowly I strolled across the wooden planks, never letting my eyes off the character that waited for me at the far end of the pier. As I got closer, I realized that this was one big, ugly cat who looked strangely familiar.

"Ahem," I said, "I believe you've got something for me!"

"That depends," the cat said in a shrill voice, "on whether you have something for us — I mean, me!"

I reached into my jacket pocket and pulled out the sack of chocolate-covered Minnow Mints. I tossed the sack into the air, then caught it in my open paw. "First

the information," I said. "Then you can have the candy."

"No way," the cat demanded. "Give me the mints, and then I'll tell you what you want to know."

"What's your name?" I asked. "I don't make deals with strangers."

"My name is Lex — ah, Lex Flabby," the cat said. "Hand over the mints."

"Don't I know you from somewhere?" I asked, dropping the sack of candy into the cat's tiny paw.

Behind me, I heard a click and the sound of little train cars squeaking on a metal track. I assumed it was one of the amusement rides shutting down for the night. I assumed wrong.

"Knock knock," whispered Frankie Fluff to Si Meeze as the cart they were hiding in began to move forward and he slipped into the entrance of The Howl of Horror.

"Who's there?" whispered Si, who had accidentally pulled the metal bar at the front of the cart down into safety position, and automatically started the ride.

"Thumping," said Frankie.

"Thumping who?"

"Thumping's making me ne—ne—nervous about this," Frankie stammered as their cart rattled into a giant wooden dog's mouth and disappeared into the darkness.

"AAAAAAAAIIIIIIIAAAAHHH!" screamed the police cats as they sped past hulking, three-eyed monster birds, beneath dripping wet spiderwebs, and along a row of mirrors that made Frankie and Si look like they had been squeezed down to the width of pencils and had heads the size of grapes.

At the end of the pier, I kept my eye on the mystery cat. He wobbled on his tiny feet and stuffed candy into his strangely rubbery mouth. If I didn't know better, I would have said that I heard a muffled voice from below, saying, "Hey, what about me? Pass some of that down here!"

"That's just my tummy growling," the cat explained, letting out a belch.

"What did you say your name was?" I asked again, with my whiskers beginning to tingle like they'd been stuck into an electric socket. Something was wrong, very wrong. I just wasn't sure yet what it was.

"Tex Tubby," the cat mumbled as he chewed noisily, "and this cheap candy is making me feel a little gassy."

"Listen, Tubby, I'm running out of patience. Tell me where I can find the Manx kittens or I'll — "

With a violent toot, the stranger let out a blast of toxic kitty-cat fart. "Whoops!" he said. The cat stumbled, and I could have sworn I heard his stomach holler, "AAARGH! I can't breathe down here!"

The cat seemed to fall apart before my eyes and become two separate cats. The one on top leaped to the ground, pulled out a little jar, and flung a mysterious powder into my face. I sneezed, and sneezed some more, and I couldn't stop. The other cat jumped up and down, screaming, "It works! It works!" as the first one searched my pockets and pulled out a big ring of keys.

Through my tears, I saw the cat pull out a pair of handcuffs and slap them around one of my wrists, and then around my ankle. I was sneezing so hard, I couldn't stop him, and before I knew it, I was completely helpless.

"Let's go, Rumpy," the first cat said to the other, and a lightbulb went off in my head as I sneezed, "Achoo! Achoo!" Rex Tabby, the greatest cat detective the world has ever known, was down — defeated by the trickiest kittens of them all, Rumpy and Stumpy Manx.

There are hundreds of ways to be bad, and there are probably hundreds of slang words for people who make a lifestyle out of being bad.

Look at the list below and find the one word that is not real cop slang for a criminal.

grifter

bindle stiff

fakeloo artist

dip

derrick

goon

sourpuss

hood

johnson brother

redhot

ANSWER

If somebody calls you a sourpuss, chances are you're just in a bad mood — not bad to the bone, like some cats we know. All of those other funny words are real cop slang for different kinds of bad guys, and it isn't funny being bad — it's just bad.

CHAPTER TEN
★ ★ ★
THE PARTY'S OVER

I had no time to lose. "TUNA! ACHOO! TUNA!"
I screamed at the top of my lungs, realizing that
something terrible must have happened to Frankie
and Si. Nobody was coming to rescue me, and nobody
was going to help me catch the Manx kittens.

Carefully, very carefully, I slipped the tip of one of
my whiskers into the keyhole of the lock that bound
my wrist, and twitched it back and forth. *CLICK!* The
lock popped open.

The other cuff dangled from my ankle, but I didn't
have time to take it off. I heard the little *pit-a-pat* of
runaway kittens echo in the distance. "Stop, in the
name of the — AAACHOOO! — law!" I shouted.

"I think we're lost," Rumpy said, as they rounded a corner and came to a stop at the foot of a high cement wall. Stumpy looked to the left. She looked to the right, where the roller coaster loomed above them.

"Climb up those bars," she said. "They lead to the top of the roller coaster. Once we get high enough, we can jump down to the other side of the wall!"

"I'm not climbing anything," Stumpy cried. "Don't you remember I'm scared of heights?"

Rumpy grabbed her brother by the scruff of his neck and pulled him onto the lower rungs.

A little rusty car blew out the exit doors of The Howl of Horror and clattered to a stop. Frankie and Si crept from the car on wobbly legs and made their way out of the gate. "Wh–wh–where's Rex?" Frankie stammered.

"Rex! REX!" Si hollered.

"Over here," I cried, "by the — AAACHOOO! — roller coaster! The mystery cat was Rumpy and Stumpy Manx, in — AAACHOOO! — disguise!"

Rumpy and Stumpy were scaling the scaffolding of the roller coaster as quickly as clowns shot out of a cannon. But when Stumpy's foot slipped and he let out a cry, I craned my neck to see the kittens hovering fifty feet above the ground.

"Don't make me come up there and get you," I shouted. "Climb on down before somebody gets hurt!"

"You'll never catch us, copper!" Rumpy laughed.

"I'm all over you," I said, "like flies on a dirty — AAACHOOO! — diaper! You troublemakers are going to spend a long time behind bars!"

I pulled myself onto the scaffolding and began climbing. Meanwhile, Rumpy and Stumpy made it to the side of the roller coaster that hung over the concrete wall. "All right, Stumpy," his sister urged, "it's time for you to jump!"

"You first!" cried Stumpy.

"No, you!" shouted Rumpy, giving her brother a big push. But Rumpy clamped his jaws onto the bar in front of him like a dog with a bone.

"You're impossible," sighed Rumpy. "If you refuse to jump, we'll have to climb up to the track and run along the top until we get to the end of the ride. Quick! Tabby's on our tail!"

"But you don't have a tail, Stumpy," Rumpy said as his sister raced upward.

When I got to the top of the roller coaster and hoisted myself up onto the track, I was gasping for breath. But my sneezing spell was over. Far ahead, I could see Rumpy and Stumpy approaching The Drop of Doom.

It was a sheer hundred-foot plunge to the bottom — the scariest and most dangerous part of the ride. Rumpy and Stumpy hesitated when they got to the edge; and that was all the time it took me to reach them.

At the entrance to the roller coaster, Si Meeze and Frankie Fluff stood by the row of empty carts that lined the track. Si flicked the switches on the control panel that operated the ride, and the track began to hum.

"We're never going to get to the top to help Rex catch the Manx kittens unless we ride the coaster," said Si.

"Ride the coaster?" moaned Frankie. "Well, I guess a little old roller coaster couldn't be any scarier than The Howl of Horror!"

"Good!" Si exclaimed. "You climb into the front cart, and I'll stay behind to operate the controls. When you get to the top, I'll shut off the power. Then you hop out, and help Rex arrest those pesky kittens!"

At the edge of The Drop of Doom, I grabbed Rumpy and Stumpy from behind and lifted them into the air. "The party's over," I growled, "and you kittens are going down."

Suddenly I heard a wild clatter coming up from behind. The roller-coaster car hurtled toward me at fifty miles an hour. "STOP!" Frankie Fluff hollered from the head of the car, but my partner, Si Meeze, wasn't able to shut off the power in time. With Rumpy and Stumpy in my arms, I leaped into the air. The cart shot under me and hurtled down The Drop of Doom.

"AAAAAAAAAAAAAARGH!" I heard voices screaming, and I think one of them was me.

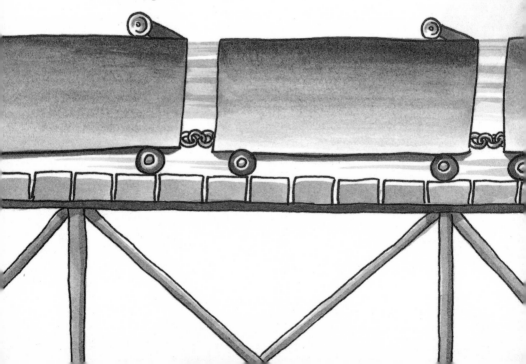

Since I'm such a nice guy, I'll let you skip class. But don't make a habit out of it! Now, go on and read Chapter Eleven, the exciting conclusion to the story!

CHAPTER ELEVEN
★★★
THE END
OF THE LINE

In midair, my tail caught the edge of a high metal bar and curled around it, leaving me hanging upside down at the top of the drop. Rumpy and Stumpy didn't care for the view. Squirming in my arms, they screamed and howled into my ears, just like their dear old Ma had taught them. Luckily I had remembered to pop in my anti-shriek earplugs!

But Rumpy had one more trick up her sleeve. She pulled out a little jar and quickly unscrewed the lid. "You can scratch us off your list, Tabby," she laughed, and shook a cloud of itching powder into the air.

In seconds, my skin began to itch like an army of fire ants were sharpening their fangs on me.

Somehow, I remembered the open handcuffs on my ankle. I squeezed Rumpy and Stumpy beneath one arm, and with my free paw I snapped the handcuffs around the pole I was dangling from.

Now that I didn't have to worry about falling to my doom, I could use my tail and my one free paw to scratch. Rumpy and Stumpy were busy scratching, too, for the itching powder covered the three of us like a white sheet. We looked like a gang of ghosts with a bad case of fleas.

Frankie's cart rolled around the length of the track. Before long he returned to the top of the roller coaster, and this time the cart rolled to a stop just short of The Drop of Doom.

"Hang on, R–R–R–R–Rex," Frankie said, looking a little green. "I'll save you!"

Frankie selected a tiny key from her enormous ring and slipped it into the lock of the handcuff. A little smile appeared on her face. "Knock knock," she said, giving the key a twist.

"Frankie," I shouted, "you've gotta be ready to catch me or — "

The lock sprang open, and I dropped like a sack of rocks, tumbling over the edge of the roller coaster. Rumpy and Stumpy were screeching and scratching, but still tucked tightly under my arm. I wasn't going to let them get away this time.

"Sorry, Rex," said Frankie, peering down from above. "I'll save that joke for later!"

We bounced off the side of the ride two or three times on our way down. Finally, with a tremendous splash, we plunged into the icy cold water that surrounded the pier. When I came up, I was choking on seaweed, with an old boot on my head.

My partner, Si, stood on the dock holding a large net. "I remember how you don't like getting wet, Rex," he explained, "so I brought this net along, just in case!"

"That's a lovely net, Si," I growled. "Next time, try using it!"

I climbed up onto the dock, and Si and I fished Rumpy and Stumpy from the river. "They look like wet rats," giggled Si.

"Hey, no harm done," I chuckled.

"This was probably the first bath they've ever had!"

I shivered and dripped with river water as cold as a polar bear's bottom, but the itching powder had washed away. How could I stay mad at my partner for long?

It was a quick ride back to the station house, with the Manx kittens locked up in the backseat. "Hey, Rumpy and Stumpy, do you want to hear something really loud?" I asked, and turned the siren all the way up.

"I can't believe we're finally going to get to see our Ma!" smiled Stumpy.

"Yeah," said Rumpy, "I guess it didn't turn out too bad. At least in prison we'll get regular meals and a clean roof over our head. Oh, and regular meals — say, do you think they have an all-you-can-eat night in jail?"

In the basement of the station house, we unlocked the door to Ma Manx's cell and tossed her kittens inside. The look on Ma's face was a twisted mixture of horror, disbelief, anger, shock, confusion, and motherly love. I never realized a cat could make so many expressions at once.

"I can't believe my tired old eyes," Ma Manx cried. "I don't know what to do first, hug you or holler at you. Oh, what the heck. Come on over here and give your Ma a kiss on the cheek — and then I'll give you a spankin' you won't forget!"

"Ma, is that your dinner tray?" Rumpy asked, racing for the greasy chow.

The captain grinned and slapped me on the shoulder. "You've done it again!" he beamed. "The Manx gang is finally behind bars, right where they belong!"

"Case closed." I smiled. "Just another day in the life of the greatest cat detective the world has ever known!"

"Oh, I almost forgot," said Frankie Fluff as she grinned and gave her anti-shriek earplugs a little twist. "Knock knock!"

"Who's there?" sighed Si.

"Gladys!"

"Gladys who?" asked the captain.

Frankie giggled, covering her mouth with her giant paw. "I'm Gladys case is over, ain't you?"

The screeching of cats fighting over their supper disappeared as we laughed, heading back up the stairs. Things were back to normal, and all was quiet in Whiskerville, U.S.A. At least, for now . . .

Well, there you have it, cats, kids, and kittens. My tale has reached its end. If you've been a student in Rex Tabby's Junior Detective School, then it's graduation time! There's only one question left to ask: Do you want more? If the answer is yes, then the adventure is just beginning.

Keep your eyes and ears open, Junior Detectives, and if you see anything funny going on, write it down. Pay attention to the details. Then give Rex Tabby a call! We've all got to work together to stop the bad guys and make the world a safer, happier place to live.

See ya around the neighborhood!